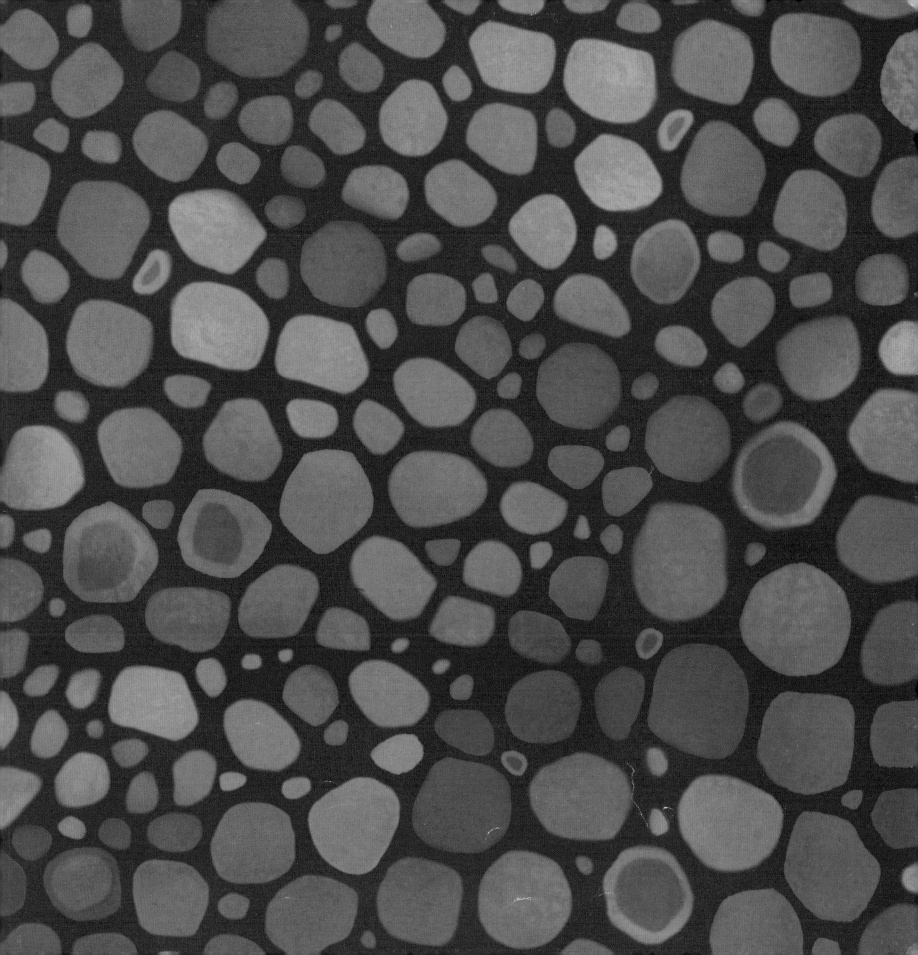

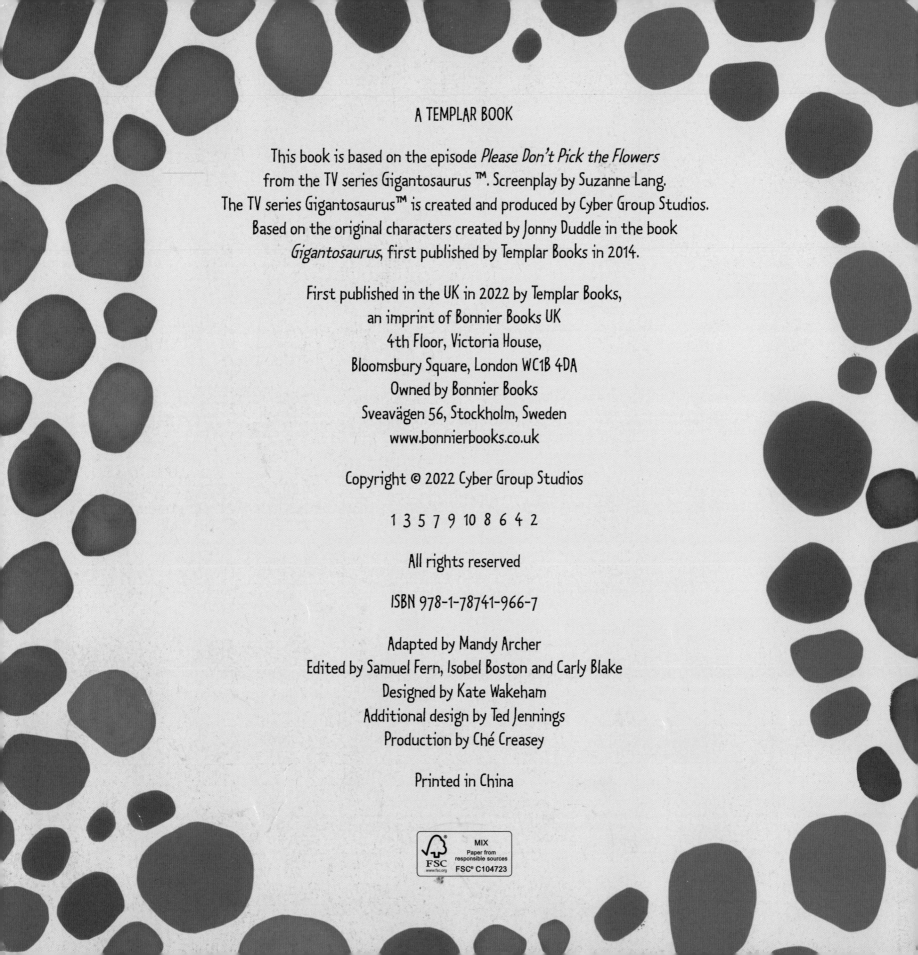

A TEMPLAR BOOK

This book is based on the episode *Please Don't Pick the Flowers*
from the TV series Gigantosaurus ™. Screenplay by Suzanne Lang.
The TV series Gigantosaurus™ is created and produced by Cyber Group Studios.
Based on the original characters created by Jonny Duddle in the book
Gigantosaurus, first published by Templar Books in 2014.

First published in the UK in 2022 by Templar Books,
an imprint of Bonnier Books UK
4th Floor, Victoria House,
Bloomsbury Square, London WC1B 4DA
Owned by Bonnier Books
Sveavägen 56, Stockholm, Sweden
www.bonnierbooks.co.uk

ISBN 978-1-78741-966-7

Adapted by Mandy Archer
Edited by Samuel Fern, Isobel Boston and Carly Blake
Designed by Kate Wakeham
Additional design by Ted Jennings
Production by Ché Creasey

Printed in China

GIGANTOSAURUS™

DINOS TO THE RESCUE

templar books

The four dinos were playing by the lake. Rocky found a smooth pebble on the beach, picked it up and threw it with all of his might. One . . . two . . . three . . . FOUR bounces!

"Yes!" cheered Rocky. "Try beating that, Bill!"

Bill shook his head. He was on lookout, because in Cretacia, trouble could strike at any moment.

Instead, Mazu took up Rocky's challenge.

"Science tells me just the right angle to throw this rock . . ." she declared.

But Mazu's rock didn't bounce – it just splashed down with a loud PLOP!

Prepare to be amazed!

No sooner had the water settled, than a huge, toothy creature reared its head out of the lake, and fixed its eyes on Mazu.

"LOOK OUT!" shouted Bill. "Termy's behind you!"

Terminonator snapped at Mazu just as she leapt to safety.

The little dinos hid until the coast was clear.
Bill was right – they DID need a lookout!

"If I hadn't listened to your warning, something terrible could have happened . . ."
Mazu gasped. Luckily, she knew just what to fetch to say thank you.

"Be back soon!" she called, dashing out of sight.

A little while later, Mazu returned with a gift for Bill.

"This is a floating flower," she said. "It's rare and should be appreciated, just like you!"

Bill nibbled a petal. "It's DELICIOUS! Have you got any more?"

"No, Bill. For dinos like us, the flowers are special once-in-a-while treats,"
Mazu explained. "The flowers grow in the swamp and are the ONLY food
the horseshoe crabs can eat."

As Mazu hurried away to work on one of her new inventions,
Bill stared down at his rumbly tummy.

"That flower was really good," he sighed. "I want more!"

Tiny frowned. "I suppose ONE more couldn't hurt."

"Come on," said Rocky. "We'll go to the swamp together!"

RUMBLE RUMBLE

Tiny, Bill and Rocky journeyed deep into the jungle,
and eventually they reached the edge of the swamp.

"We must be near the floating flower bush now," said Tiny.

Bill took a running jump off a giant leaf . . . straight into a pool of QUICKSAND!

Luckily, a friendly horseshoe crab was passing and lifted Bill up out of danger. Rocky and Tiny hopped on too.

Tiny spotted the bush just up ahead on a mud bank. There were lots of horseshoe crabs gathered around it. They were eating the flowers, just like Mazu said.

"Look, there are plenty of flowers!" Bill said, and rushed over to pick some.

Thanks, horseshoe crab! Let's go!

Bill hadn't been at the flower bush long, when two archaeopteryxes landed beside him.

"What are they doing?" wondered Rocky, looking on.

Tiny shrugged. "It looks like they're picking something off the horseshoes' shells."

Horseshoes have great taste!

With an armful of flowers, Bill waded back to the others.

Tiny's face fell when she saw all of the flowers Bill was carrying.

"Why have you got so many?" she asked. "Mazu said that the horseshoe crabs need them."

They've got plenty!

Rocky swallowed a petal. "They are really yummy!" he agreed.

Tiny sighed. If everyone else was eating them, it must be OK for her to try just one . . .

"Oh wow," she cried. "I LOVE THEM!"

When they got home, Mazu couldn't believe her eyes.

"Oh Bill!" she said. "I wouldn't have given you a flower if I knew you'd take MORE!"

Bill didn't understand, so Mazu pulled down a chart to explain.

The horseshoes climb onto the mud bank to eat the flowers . . .

"While the crabs eat, archaeopteryxes pick molluscs off their backs . . .

Then the archies fly over the savannah and drop the mollusc shells . . .

Rugo uses the shells to dig up bones . . .

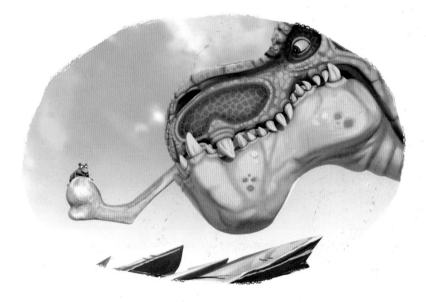

. . . and eats them with Giganto!"

"Every flower and animal depends on each other," Mazu explained. "This is called an 'ecosystem'. Every part has to help, or nothing will work at all."

Mazu's friends were shocked. Who knew that such a little flower could be so important?

"We have to take them back, don't we?" said Bill, hanging his head.

"At least we didn't pick ALL the flowers," Rocky reminded him. "There are still some left."

Mazu sighed with relief. "The horseshoe crabs should be fine for now, but we should take the flowers back tomorrow."

They all agreed. The crabs needed the flowers much more than they did!

The next morning, the little dinos heard a commotion outside the den. Rugo and Archie were searching for food.

"Oh no!" said Mazu. "Rugo can't find shells because Archie can't find molluscs, so that means the horseshoe crabs aren't eating the flowers!"

"If Rugo can't dig up bones, what will Giganto eat?" cried Bill.

Just then, the earth began to shake. BOOM! BOOM! BOOM!

ROOOAAAARRR!

Gigantosaurus stormed into view,
HUNGRIER and ANGRIER than ever.

"If he doesn't find a bone soon,"
Mazu shouted, "he's going to tear up
Cretacia looking for one! We need
to fix the ecosystem!"

"Come on!" said Bill, kneeling beside Rugo. "Let's find a bone for Giganto!"

The little dinos started digging as fast as they could. At last, they found a perfect bone.

"I'll give it to Giganto," said Rocky.

"No! I should do it," Bill insisted. "This is all my fault."

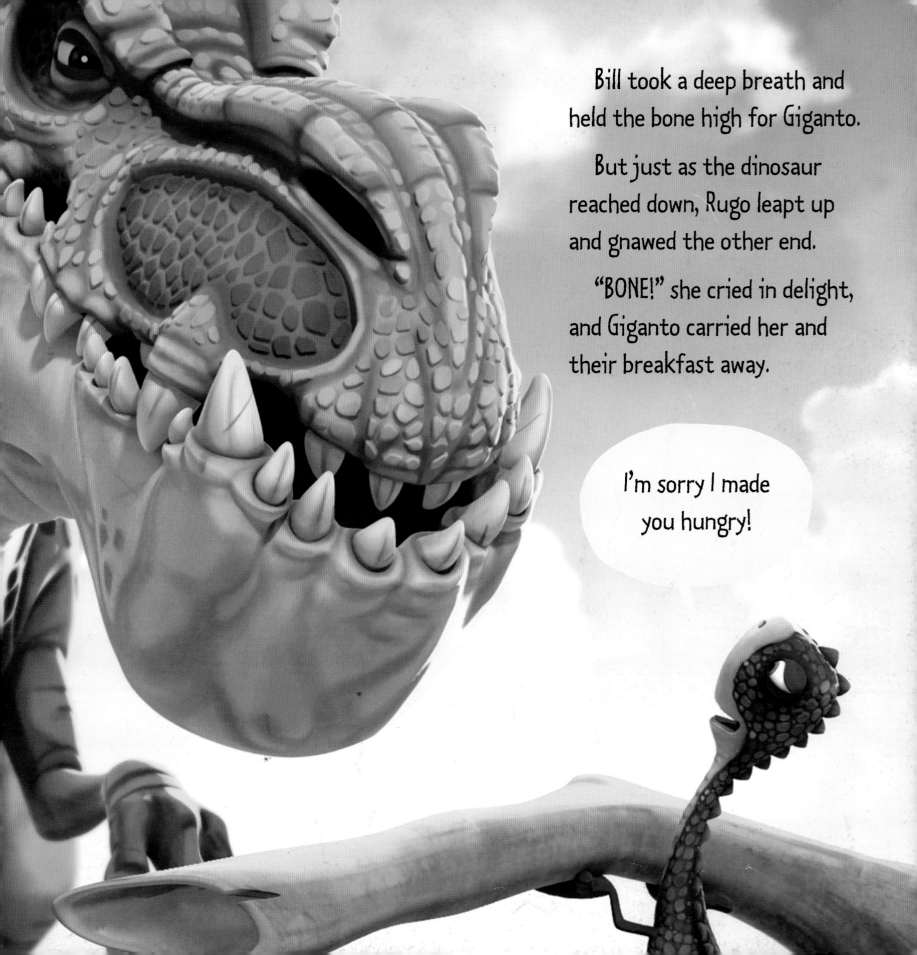

Bill took a deep breath and held the bone high for Giganto.

But just as the dinosaur reached down, Rugo leapt up and gnawed the other end.

"BONE!" she cried in delight, and Giganto carried her and their breakfast away.

I'm sorry I made you hungry!

The friends gathered the rest of the flowers and hurried back to the swamp.

"Oh no!" cried Bill when he saw the bush. "All the flowers from the lower branches are gone!"

Bill quickly gave the crabs the flowers they were carrying.

Hey, horseshoes! Come and eat!

"Phew! It's working!" said Bill.

"But once they're done with these, they'll have nothing to eat if they can't reach the top of the bush!" explained Mazu.

The little dinos sprung into action, and tied the bush down so that the crabs could reach every flower.

"Look!" yelled Rocky. "The flying archies are back!"

The archaeopteryxes swooped down and started to feed on the molluscs.

"The ecosystem . . ." whispered Tiny. "It's coming back to life!"

Bill spotted some purple dots lying on the ground. "Those must be the flower seeds."

He collected them up, then carefully started scattering them over the mud.

Mazu beamed. More seeds meant more flowers for the horseshoe crabs!

"I just wish I could throw them further," sighed Bill.

Suddenly, a dark shadow fell over the swamp . . .

"Hi, Giganto," Bill whimpered, clutching his precious collection of seeds. Giganto slowly breathed in, sucking the seeds into his enormous nostrils.

Then, with one ear-splitting SNEEZE, he blasted the seeds – and Bill – across the swamp.

Bill landed safely in the
bushes with his friends.

"Look, Bill!" Mazu cried.

All around the swamp, hundreds of flower
seeds were gliding down into the mud. In time,
the swamp would heal and there would be plenty
of food for everyone.

Giganto swished his tail and stomped away.

"You know, I've realised that Giganto and I have two things in common," Bill told the others. "We can both help the ecosystem . . . and we both get hungry!"

You are ALWAYS hungry!

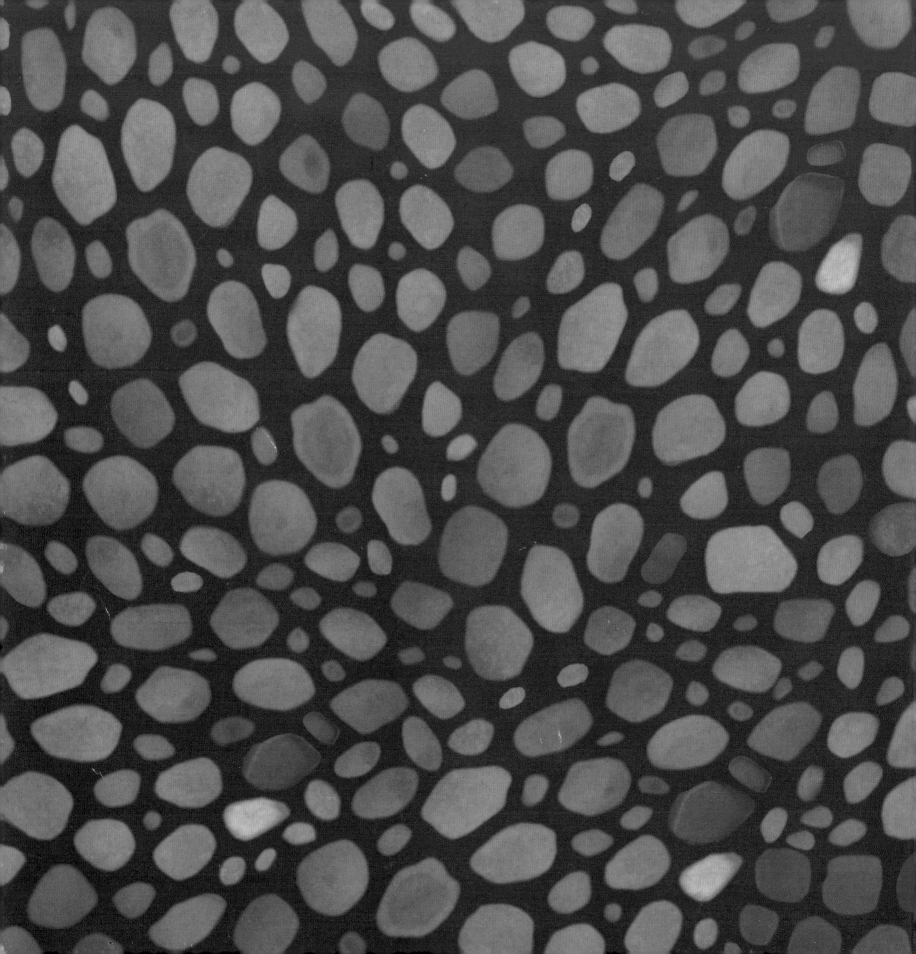

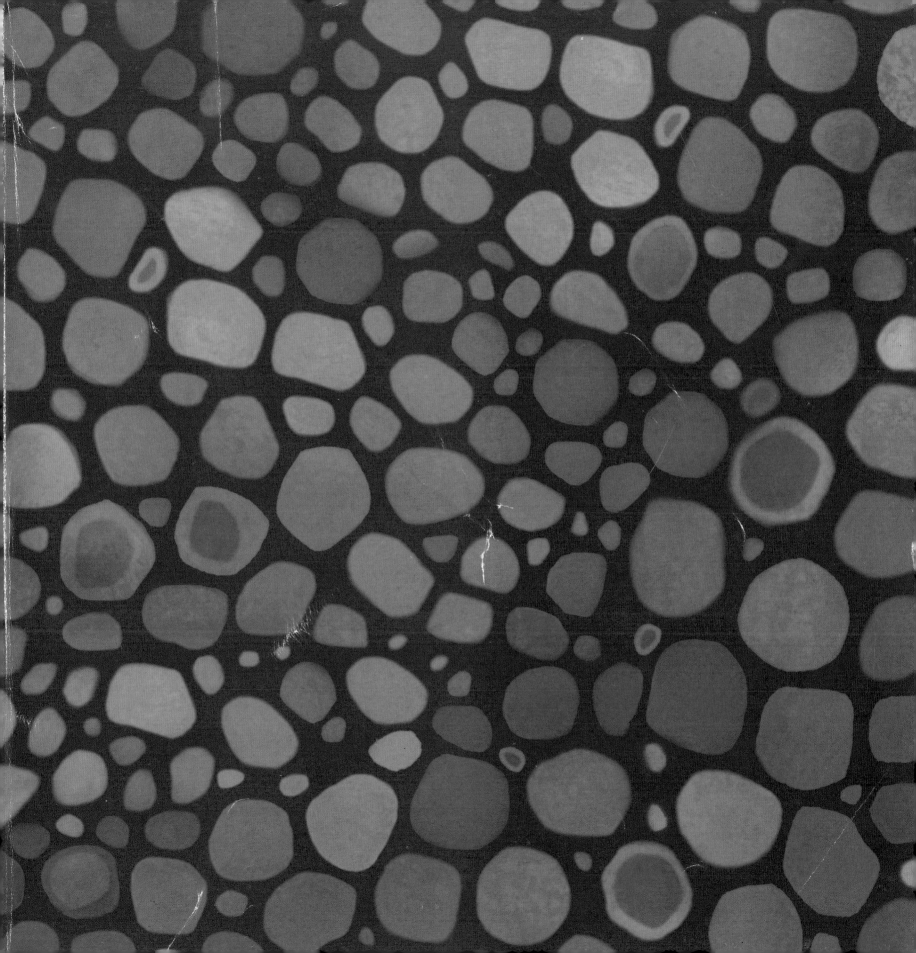

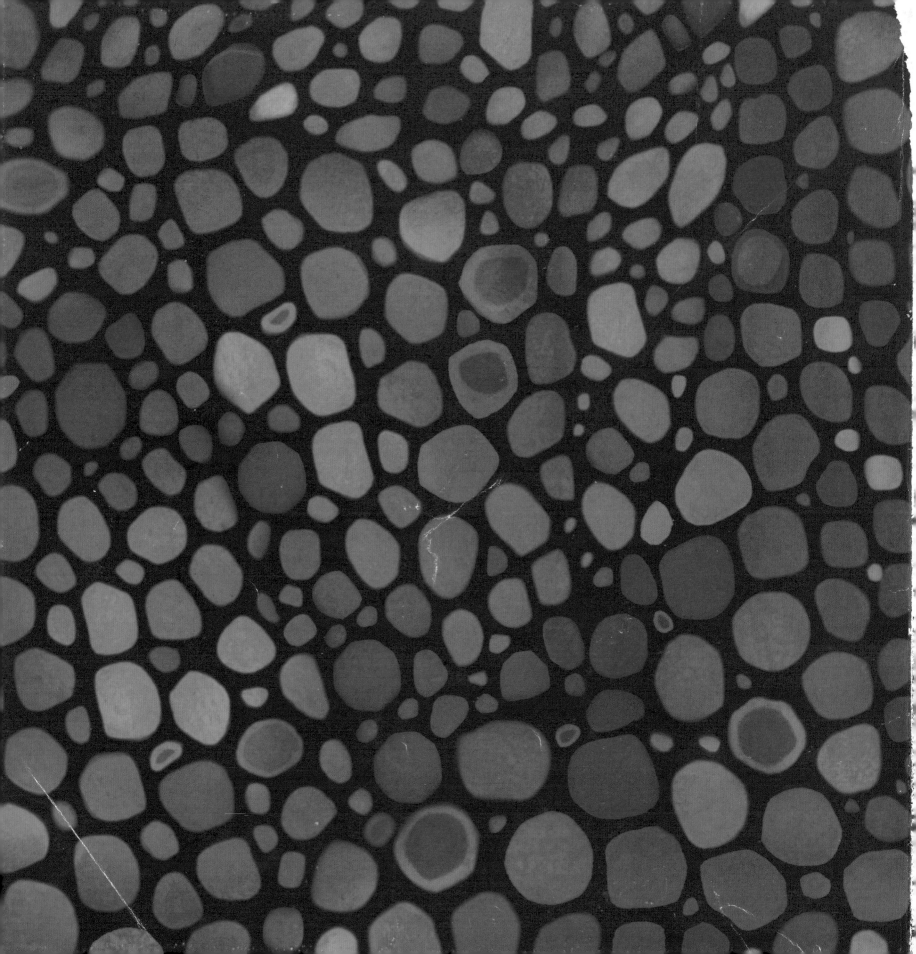